To my father, Manuel J. Tavares

The author would like to thank Lennie Merullo, Kirk Carapezza,
Cord Tocci, Kara LaReau, Caroline Lawrence, Chris Paul, Christopher Bing,
Kevin McCarthy, Mark Schlenker, David Hall, Rosemary Stimola,
and special thanks to Sarah K. Tavares.

First edition 2004

Library of Congress Cataloging-in-Publication Data

Tavares, Matt.
Oliver's Game / Matt Tavares. —1st ed.
p.   cm.
Summary: Oliver's grandfather tells him the story of how
he almost joined the Chicago Cubs baseball team.
ISBN 0-7636-1852-7
[1. Baseball—Fiction. 2. Grandfathers—Fiction.
3. Chicago Cubs (Baseball team)—Fiction.] I. Title.
PZ7.T211427 Hal 2004
[E]—dc21   2002025991

2 4 6 8 10 9 7 5 3 1

Printed in China

This book was typeset in Bodoni Antiqua.
The illustrations were done in pencil and watercolor.

Candlewick Press
2067 Massachusetts Avenue
Cambridge, Massachusetts 02140

visit us at www.candlewick.com

Oliver's Game

MATT TAVARES

CANDLEWICK PRESS
CAMBRIDGE, MASSACHUSETTS

Oliver Hall loved baseball. He loved helping out at Hall's Nostalgia, his grandfather's store. And he loved listening to Grandpa Hall's wonderful stories about what he called the Golden Age of the Game. Grandpa told Oliver about the last time the Cubs made it to the World Series, and about great players like "Swish" Nicholson and "Hack" Wilson.

"Every item in this shop has a story to tell," Grandpa Hall would say.

◆ ◆ ◆

One day, a customer called and asked for a 1945 World Series program.

"We'll take a look and call you back if we find one," said Grandpa. "Oliver, could you check the closet?"

Oliver rummaged through several cartons marked 1940s, then noticed an old wooden box behind them. He opened it. Inside, he found a Chicago Cubs uniform.

"Wow!" he said. "Grandpa, whose uniform is this? Charlie Root's? Billy Herman's?"

"It's mine," Grandpa Hall said.

"But you never played for the Cubs," said Oliver. "How could it be yours?"

Grandpa smiled. "I've wanted to tell you about this uniform for a long time. It's a very special story, though it's not always a happy one. Are you sure you're ready to hear it?"

"I'm ready," Oliver said. "Tell me, Grandpa! Please?"

"All right, then," said Grandpa Hall. "Let's see . . . this story begins in September of 1941, during the Golden Age of the Game. . . ."

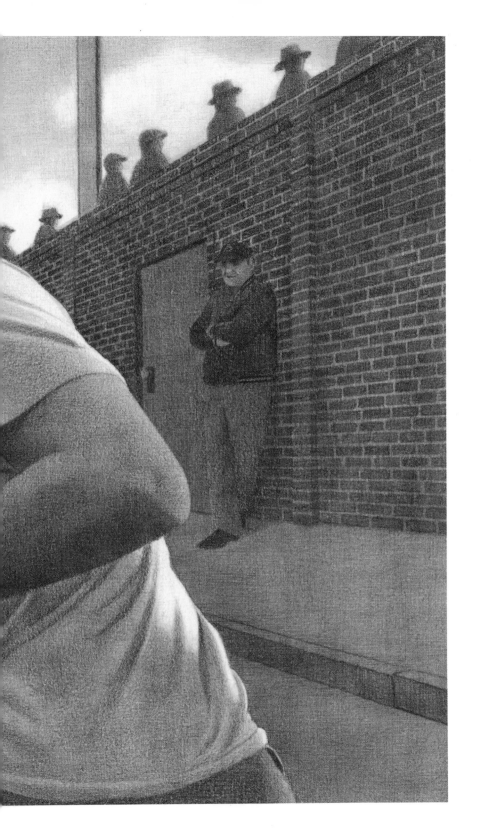

I WAS EIGHTEEN YEARS OLD, and it was the end of baseball season. Inside the ballpark, the Cubs were getting ready to play the Cardinals. I was out in front of my house, playing stickball with my friends, like I did every Saturday.

That morning, I hit a home run that soared all the way past Clark Street. I hustled around the bases and crossed home plate.

"Nice one, kid!" a man said, reaching out to shake my hand. "I'm Jimmie Wilson, manager of the Cubs."

"Thanks," I answered. "I'm Oliver Hall."

"You're quite a hitter," Mr. Wilson said. "How would you like to practice with the team?"

"Wow—I'd love to!" I replied.

"Well, follow me," he said.

We went into the Cubs' clubhouse, and Mr. Wilson handed me a uniform.

"Meet me on the field when you're ready," he said.

• • •

I'll always remember the moment I walked out of the dugout and set foot on the grass. I had been inside the ballpark many times before, but never on the field. It was like a dream.

"Let's go, Oliver!" my friends cheered from the rooftop of my house.

"Hey, rookie!" Mr. Wilson hollered from the pitcher's mound. "Head out to left and shag some flies!"

The first batter blasted a deep drive right over my head. I dove for it, but I was so nervous that I tripped over my own feet. I heard some of the other players laughing at me as I got up and brushed the dirt off my uniform.

I made sure not to miss the next one.

After a few batters, Mr. Wilson turned toward me.

"Hey, rookie!" he hollered. "You're up!"

I jogged to the dugout and grabbed a bat.

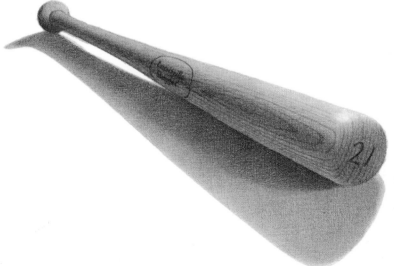

As I stepped up to the plate, I heard voices from around the batting cage.

"Who's the rookie?" yelled one player.

"Where'd they get this kid?" scoffed another.

Mr. Wilson wound up, and as the ball left his hand, I focused and swung the heavy wooden bat as hard as I could. A shock ran up my arms as the bat struck the ball head on— it soared over the left field bleachers, toward the street where I had played stickball earlier that morning.

After that, I didn't hear any more from the other players. A crowd gathered around the batting cage to watch me hit.

After batting practice, Mr. Wilson let me watch the game from the dugout.

"You're the best hitter I've seen in a long time," he told me.

"Thanks, Mr. Wilson," I answered.

"We're gonna need a new left fielder next spring," he said. "How would you like to try out for us?"

"I sure would!" I exclaimed.

"Okay, kid," he said, "I'll see what I can do about getting you invited to spring training."

◆ ◆ ◆

The Cubs beat the Cardinals that day, and for those nine glorious innings, I felt like a big leaguer.

When the game was over, Mr. Wilson said, "Keep the uniform, rookie. You may need it next season!"

I ran home to tell all my friends. All I had ever wanted was to play for the Cubs, and now my dream was coming true.

But two months later, everything changed.

On December 7, Japan attacked Pearl Harbor, in Hawaii. Suddenly, America was at war.

◆   ◆   ◆

For the first time in my life, baseball didn't seem very important. In the newspaper, I read about battles being fought in places I'd never heard of. In the sports pages, instead of articles about the Cubs preparing for another baseball season, I read about my heroes heading off to war. I tried to imagine myself playing ball while other people were fighting a war, but I just couldn't do it. So on December 11, I joined the Marines.

My platoon was sent to a place called Guadalcanal in August of 1942. We were fighting along the Tenaru River when a grenade exploded in my bunker.

I was lucky to make it out of there alive. But the doctors soon told me that I would never play ball again.

◆   ◆   ◆

When I finally got home to Chicago, Mr. Wilson called. "We're all proud of you, rookie," he said. "Anytime you want to join us in the dugout, you're always welcome."

I went to the game the next day, but being in the dugout just didn't feel the same. It made me sad to be so close to my dream. After that, I stayed away from Wrigley Field.

In 1945, the war ended. That same year, the Cubs made it to the World Series. I started watching games again from the rooftop—including game six, when the Cubs won it in the bottom of the twelfth! The whole ballpark went crazy!

And that's when it finally dawned on me: The game of baseball is more than just the players on the field. Everyone is a part of it, from the guy selling hot dogs to the fans in the grandstand. So even though I wasn't playing left field, I was still a part of the game. And baseball was still a part of me.

A few years later, I opened Hall's Nostalgia, in the very house where I grew up, across the street from my favorite place in the world.

"After the war, I packed my uniform up and stored it away," Grandpa Hall said. "I think it hurt too much to see it. But now, I feel proud and lucky to have worn it—even if it was for only nine innings. Want to try it on?"

Oliver carefully zipped up the jersey. "Wow," he said, "I feel like I'm in the big leagues."

"I want you to have it," said Grandpa, "now that you know what it means to wear it."

Oliver's eyes widened. "Are you sure?"

"I don't need it anymore," Grandpa said with a smile. "I'll always be part of the game. And so will you."

Across the street, the Cubs were finishing up batting practice.

"Let's go upstairs," Grandpa said. "Our game is just about to start."

From the rooftop, Oliver and Grandpa heard the umpire yell, "Play ball!" as the Cubs took the field. A triumphant roar rose from the grandstand.

"My favorite place in the world," said Grandpa.

"Mine too," said Oliver.